BILLY SLATER
PRESENTS
TRY
TIME

A Random House book
Published by Random House Australia Pty Ltd
Level 3, 100 Pacific Highway, North Sydney NSW 2060
www.randomhouse.com.au

First published by Random House Australia in 2014

Addresses for companies within the Random House Group can be found at www.randomhouse.com.au/offices

National Library of Australia
Cataloguing-in-Publication Entry

Author: Loughlin, Patrick.
Title: Try time / Patrick Loughlin, with contributions from Billy Slater;
illustrated by Nahum Ziersch.
ISBN: 978 0 85798 246 9 (pbk)
Series: Billy Slater; 1.
Target Audience: For primary school age.
Subjects: Rugby League football – Juvenile fiction.
Rugby League football players – Juvenile fiction.
Other Authors/Contributors: Slater, Billy; Ziersch, Nahum, illustrator.
Dewey Number: A823.4

Illustration and design by Nahum Ziersch
Typeset by Midland Typesetters, Australia
Printed in Australia by Griffin Press, an accredited ISO AS/NZS 14001:2004 Environmental Management System printer

Random House Australia uses papers that are natural, renewable and recyclable products and made from wood grown in sustainable forests. The logging and manufacturing processes are expected to conform to the environmental regulations of the country of origin.

BILLY SLATER

PRESENTS

TRY TIME

WRITTEN BY

PATRICK LOUGHLIN

ILLUSTRATED BY

NAHUM ZIERSCH

RANDOM HOUSE AUSTRALIA

BILLY SLATER

When I started playing footy, I wasn't only focused on scoring tries (as much fun as it was). I just wanted to have fun. And I still do. To score a try takes hard work and, a lot of the time, the help of your teammates.

Your teammates are the ones who will give you a pat on the back when you have done a great job and they'll also be the first ones to encourage you when you make an error. At the end of the day, it's about running onto the footy field, getting involved and having a lot of fun.

Sometimes, though, things won't go your way and you'll have to work through it. There have been times when I've tried my hardest to catch the ball or kick it a little bit further and, for some reason or another, it didn't work out. But that's okay, as long as you take a minute to remember that you gave it your best shot and you'll give it another try.

In *Try Time*, you will read about how Josh tries and tries to succeed, but something is slightly off. Maybe he's trying too hard or maybe it's just not for him. He needs a little help on the way to see it through and to enjoy his footy.

I hope you enjoy reading *Try Time* and understand that, while winning is great, being part of a team and having fun is often a lot better. It's also important to share your feelings with others around you – especially your family – as they are often the best people to help you out.

Billy Slater

1
UP AND AT 'EM

THOOOWEEEEEP!

The ref's whistle blew to start the first half. The West Hill Ravens received the ball from the kick-off and immediately began hitting it up against the opposition.

Josh Brown stood out on the right wing in his very first game of rugby league, poised for the perfect pass that would send him over the line for a try.

He had been waiting his whole life for a chance to step onto a real football ground and play in his first footy team, and now his time had come. He was ready.

Josh stood, steely-eyed and determined, watching his teammates work the ball out of their half.

Tackle one: a nice hit-up.

Tackle two: a short bust.

Tackle three: a lovely off-load. Now, a genuine break – they had broken through the opposition's defence!

The Ravens worked the ball from right to left across the line. Josh was running alongside his centre, following the action, ready for his first touch of the ball.

'Out wide!' cried the inside centre. 'Pass it out wide!'

Josh could feel his heart pounding in

anticipation. *Here it comes.* The next thing he knew, the centre had the ball. 'I'm here!' yelled Josh.

His teammate nodded and, drawing in two of the opposition, floated a pass out to Josh.

Josh caught the ball and sprinted away like a racehorse down the sideline. It was a glorious feeling. He could feel the wind in his face and hair. He was a blur. A lightning strike. A speeding bullet. He'd never felt so fast.

With the tryline in sight, there was just the fullback and the winger to beat. But Josh was too fast for them. No one would catch him. He was so fast the fullback and the winger were laughing.

Hang on, why are they laughing? Josh wondered.

All of a sudden he felt a little cold. The wind wasn't just in his face and hair, it was buffeting his whole body. Josh glanced down and realised he wasn't wearing his jersey. *I must have forgotten to put it on*, he thought. *It doesn't matter now, I can put it on after I score a try.*

Only metres from the tryline, he could hear the crowd roaring with excitement. Except it didn't sound like excitement. It was more like laughter.

Josh looked down again and realised it wasn't just his jersey that was missing – he had no shorts on. He was running down the sideline in his first-ever game of rugby league in his football boots, green-and-black Ravens socks and a rather small, tight-fitting pair of Superman undies that he hadn't worn since he was five.

Josh stopped running and turned to look behind him. The whole crowd and both teams were in hysterics. Everyone was pointing and whistling.

Josh tried to cover himself with the ball, but that just made everyone laugh even more. The ref was laughing so hard he could barely blow his whistle. When he finally did, he signalled a penalty.

'Penalty against the Ravens. Player out of uniform,' the ref said, giving Josh a wink.

Hang on, he looks familiar. Josh squinted at the ref. 'Grandad?'

EST HILL PARK

'Up and at 'em!' yelled the ref.

Josh opened his eyes to find his grandad's large red face smiling down at him.

'Come on, Joshie. Up and at 'em.'

Phew, thought Josh, *it was just a dream.*

'Big day today. First game of the season,' said Grandad.

A sudden flood of panic filled Josh's ten-year-old body. His grandad was right. It *was* the first game of the season.

'Let's go, kiddo,' said Grandad, whipping off Josh's doona and exposing his skinny limbs to the cool morning air. 'You don't want to be late for your first game, do you?'

But for some strange reason, Josh found himself unable to move.

2 FIRST-GAME JITTERS

Ten minutes later Josh was sitting at the kitchen table, staring into a bowl of porridge. It hadn't taken him long to get ready, once he'd managed to peel himself out of bed.

After throwing on a T-shirt and his hoodie, Josh had triple-checked that he was wearing his new Ravens footy shorts and a pair of plain blue undies – not his Superman ones (which had long since disappeared from his drawer, anyway). Then he packed his new football boots, shoulder pads and mouthguard into his backpack. Within minutes he was ready for his first game of football.

Josh had been waiting for this moment for weeks, ever since player registration in February. Now the season was finally here, he knew he should be feeling excited. After all, he had practically begged his mum to let him join the team.

Josh, his dad and footy-mad grandad had worked together all summer to wear down Josh's mum. She'd thought he was too young and too small for rugby league and had suggested he'd be better off playing soccer, where he was less likely to get hurt.

But for Josh, it was league or nothing. It was *his* game.

So why did he feel like a herd of elephant-sized butterflies had just stampeded through his stomach? The nervous feeling only increased the longer Josh stared at his porridge.

'Josh, eat your breakfast,' said Mum, while wiping down the kitchen bench. She poured herself a cup of tea and sat down across from him. 'Oats are low GI and very nutritious, and the bananas will give you the energy you need for your first big game.'

Chloe, Josh's baby sister, seemed to agree. She was happily smearing porridge all over her face and highchair. But Josh wasn't so sure.

'I really wish I could be there today,' his mum continued. 'But your sister's teething and I need to get to the chemist before they shut.'

Chloe seems fine to me, thought Josh. He looked at his sister, who was happily drooling all over her own hand while blowing porridge and spit bubbles through her mouth and nose at the same time. Josh winced in disgust.

'Not hungry, lad?' asked Grandad. 'Only natural to have a few first-game jitters. You'll be fine once you run onto the field. I always was.'

Josh nodded and brought another spoonful to his mouth. But something inside his stomach shuddered, and a moment later he was rushing off to the toilet.

3
A BEAUTIFUL DAY FOR FOOTY

The ground was buzzing with activity. There were three games of mini-league on and a growing crowd of spectators was setting up folding chairs and blankets on the grassy slope beside the football field. The smell of sausages and onions sizzling on the barbecue wafted through the crisp April air.

It was a beautiful day for football.

Despite his nerves, Josh couldn't help but feel excited. He ran over to join his teammates and Coach Steve for some light passing drills and warm-up exercises. After fifteen minutes, the team huddled before the kick-off.

'All right, boys. It's the first game of the season, let's not be shy out there,' said Coach Steve.

He was a tall man with a shiny bald head that he usually kept covered with a battered old Ravens cap. All the boys liked him because he was tough but fair and used funny expressions.

'We're up against the Harbourside Hawks today. These guys were in the top four last year and they've got some big, tough forwards and lightning-quick backs. So, we've got to be ready for anything.'

‘I’m confused, Coach,’ said the Ravens five-eighth and team clown, Tai Nguyen. ‘When you say “ready for anything”, do you mean like an alien invasion or something?’

‘No, Tai, I don’t mean an alien invasion. I mean you need to get on that field and play your heart out. And before you ask, yes, I want to see your heart actually pop out and take a break on the bench while you keep running,’ said Coach Steve.

The whole team laughed.

Josh found out exactly how tough the Hawks were when he tried to tackle one of them. The Hawks player just palmed him off like he was a piece of soft cheese. But when Josh hit the ground he didn’t feel like

soft cheese. His bones jarred and the thud vibrated through his entire body.

'Up you get, Josh! Don't let that big lout stop you,' yelled Grandad.

Josh pushed himself up off the ground and brushed his grass-stained elbows and knees. He jogged back into the line, a little worse for wear.

The good thing about playing on the wing was that it meant you didn't have to do a lot of tackling, because most of the action tended to happen in the middle of the field. Eventually, though, someone would run your way. You always had to be ready.

With each play of the ball, Josh ran up in the defensive line, ready to meet the attack. But he could feel that hard ground biting at his football boots with every step. The ground felt like it would eat him alive, one skinned knee at a time.

The Hawks worked the ball out wide and, suddenly, Josh had a large centre steaming towards him. He closed his eyes and threw himself into the tackle. This time he was slightly more successful. He managed to bring down the player . . . right on top of him.

It took Josh a little longer to get to his feet. His head had connected with the player's knee and was still ringing like a church bell on Sunday.

'That's it, Josh! Good tackle!' yelled Grandad. 'Next time try using your shoulders more and your face less.'

Josh was starting to find his grandad's encouraging sideline comments slightly discouraging. And when the Ravens finally got the ball, they were downright distracting.

'Come on, Ravens. Run straight!'

'Let's go, Ravens. Spread it wide!'

'Pass it to the wing, ya bunch of ball hogs!'

Josh could feel the rest of the team glaring at him. Maybe that was why no one had passed him the ball in the entire first half.

THOOOWEEEEEP!

Josh looked up at the scoreboard. The Ravens were down 6–0 and he was yet to touch the ball. It wasn't quite the start to the season he'd been hoping for.

4
BUTTER-FINGERS

'Listen, we're only down by six points,' said Coach Steve. He looked at the boys sitting in a semicircle around him eating orange quarters. 'There's still plenty of time in the game. Let's watch our passes and support the man with the ball.'

'It might be a bit easier to concentrate on passing if *someone's* grandad wasn't yelling at us the whole time,' said Corey.

Josh looked down at his orange peel.

Corey was the outside centre and a

great player, but Josh had a feeling Corey didn't like him. Maybe it was the death stares Corey kept giving him, or the way he had walked up to Josh on the first day of training and said, 'Stay out of my way, newbie!'

Now it was becoming clear that Corey didn't like Josh's grandad's sideline comments, either. Josh couldn't blame him. His grandad took footy very seriously.

'Well, it wouldn't hurt you to pass it once in a while, Corey,' Coach Steve said cheerily.

Corey shot a fiery look at Josh. 'But . . .'

'No buts. It's our first game of the season, let's have some fun. I want to see everyone involved and having a run with the ball,' said

Coach Steve. He winked at Josh. 'Now, let's get out there and put some points on that board!'

When the second half began, it seemed as if Coach Steve's talk had worked. The Ravens got off to a flying start, receiving the ball from the kick-off. Cameron Cotter, their fullback, took the ball on the full and broke through the Hawks' defence.

Two tackles later, Tai got a razor-sharp cut-out pass to Corey, who took off through a yawning gap on the Hawks' left side. Josh went with him in support but Corey was too fast, racing away to score under the posts. The Ravens halfback and captain, Liam McGill, converted the try to lock the score at 6–6. The team celebrated the first try of the season with an excited bout of high fives.

But their great start hit a snag a few minutes later when the Ravens' big prop forward, Lucas 'Poppa' Popovic, came charging in for a run and knocked the ball on in the very first tackle.

'Hold onto the ball, Ravens!' hollered a familiar voice from the sidelines.

'Doesn't your grandad ever stop yelling, Brown?' snarled Corey.

Josh didn't reply.

The next ten minutes was all Hawks. They kept the Ravens pinned in their own half, and it wasn't long before the Hawks went over the line again.

'Chins up, Ravens! Get it together out there.' This time it was Coach Steve yelling some encouragement as the team stood behind the posts.

They watched the Hawks goal kicker easily slot the ball over the black dot for another two points.

As the second half wore on, the game turned into an arm wrestle, with neither team able to score. The tension rose and the Ravens crowd began chanting. Josh relaxed a little. At least now it wasn't just his grandad calling out from the sideline.

Josh felt a bit like a spectator himself.

He seemed to be doing a lot of running around and watching things happen. He tried to help out but he always arrived too late.

When the Ravens had the ball Josh made sure to run up with the line, but the ball never seemed to make it out to the wing. In a way, Josh didn't mind. He was a little worried about what might happen if the ball ever was passed to him.

THOOOWEEEEEP!

'Forward pass,' announced the ref, awarding the Ravens a penalty.

'Let's go, boys,' called Coach Steve, clapping from the sideline.

Josh looked up at the scoreboard.

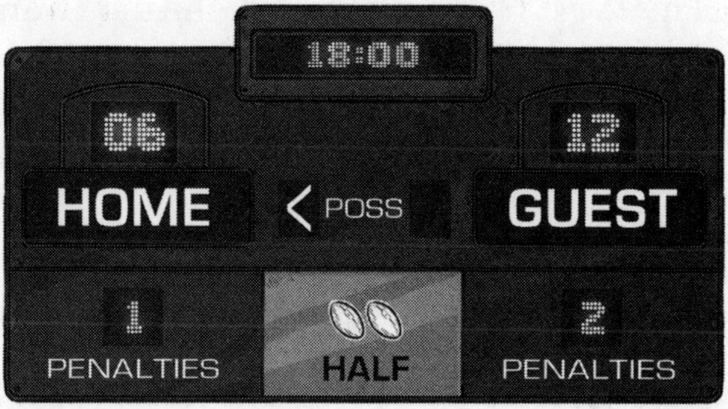

They were down by a try. With two minutes to go before full-time, this was the Ravens' last chance to score. They had to work the ball out wide and go for a try in the corner.

It was finally Josh's chance to get involved. So why did he feel like throwing up? *No time to worry about that now*, thought Josh. *It's time to play footy.*

THOOOWEEEEEP!

The West Hill Ravens took the tap twenty metres out from the tryline.

Here it comes. The ball is coming to me. Any second now.

Azza passed it to Tai, who dummied and twirled and off-loaded to the Ravens' go-to tackle-buster, Junior Taafuli.

Fifteen metres.

Junior smashed through the Hawks defence, taking two of their defenders with him, and got an easy off-load to Cameron Cotter.

Ten metres.

Cameron accelerated through a gap and flicked a sneaky pass back to Blake 'the Fake' Vargas, the Ravens inside centre. Blake turned to find Corey cutting through

on his right and Josh running outside him on the left.

Five metres.

'Pass it out wide!' Grandad shouted from the sideline.

Blake seemed to hear him because he did pass the ball out wide. It was a terrific pass. It floated towards Josh as if on a breeze. All Josh had to do was pluck it from the air and dive over the tryline.

Two metres.

Josh raised his hands to catch the ball. The crowd of parents and onlookers roared. The ball touched his fingertips. Josh felt its hard yellow hide slide into his grasp as he dived for the line. The crowd gasped. He was over! He was over the line!

Unfortunately, the ball wasn't.

Josh watched helplessly as it bounced over the dead-ball line. He had fumbled it right at the last second.

The crowd went silent.

Then came the sound that would haunt Josh for days: a single loud, long 'Boooooooooo!'

'Good one, butter-fingers. Can't you even catch a ball?' Corey muttered, walking past him. 'He should have passed it to me.'

The final whistle sounded and Josh's team left the field, their heads down.

Josh's head hung lower than all the rest. The Ravens had lost the first game of the season and it was all his fault.

5
SAUSAGES AND STARRY SKIES

Later that night Josh still couldn't get the game out of his mind. All he could see was that yellow football slipping out of his hands while Corey's words echoed in his ears.

Can't you even catch a ball?

It put him right off his favourite dinner of sausages and mashed potato. Not that the meal looked that appetising. The sausages were grey and shrivelled and the mashed potato was cold and lumpy.

The annoying thing was that Josh *could*

catch a ball. When he played footy in the playground at school or out in the street he had no problem holding onto a pass. Even at training he had rarely dropped a pass. So, why couldn't he do it when he really needed to?

'Still thinking about the game?' asked Mum.

Josh shrugged.

'Never mind, there'll be plenty of other games for you to score a try in,' she said, offering her best Caring Mum smile. 'Eat up. A full stomach will make you feel better.'

Josh looked down at his plate again. 'These sausages look a bit . . . weird.'

His mother's face tightened into a frown. 'I had to cook them in the pan because

I couldn't get the gas on the barbecue to work.'

'Oh.'

Josh's dad usually cooked the sausages on the barbecue and they were always golden-brown and juicy. But he was away, working interstate. Josh knew his mum wasn't happy about it. Sometimes, when he was in bed, he could hear her arguing with his dad on the phone.

'What about Grandad? Couldn't he –'

'He's gone out to the club with his bowls team,' his mum said sharply.

'Oh.'

The awkward silence was broken by a familiar sound in the Brown household.

'Waaaaaaahhhhhh!'

Josh's mum sighed. 'There's your sister, right on schedule. If you don't want your dinner, scrape your plate into the dog's bowl, then throw it in the dishwasher. I need to feed Chloe.'

'Sure.' Josh watched his mum leave the room. 'No problem.'

He gave his sausage to their big, black and ever-hungry Labrador, Harry, and placed his plate in the dishwasher. Then he plonked down on the sofa, just in time for the last half of the game. It had been the same every night lately. With Dad away and his mum busy with Chloe, Josh always ended up in front of the telly alone.

'Fifth and last. Up goes the bomb. It's a high one, but Billy Slater is there to take it . . .' a commentator yelled with excitement.

'Yep, no doubt about it – Billy Slater is as safe as houses,' said another commentator.

Billy Slater was Josh's favourite player. He never dropped the ball under pressure and he was great at making breaks as well.

I wonder how he does it, thought Josh.

'Now Slater has it. He beats one, he beats two, he beats the fullback and he's over to score! What a try! Simply amazing work from the fullback!'

Amazing. Josh wondered if he would ever do anything amazing in a game. He was interrupted by a sudden jolt against his leg. It was Harry shoving him with his nose. 'Wanna go out, boy?'

Josh opened the door and let Harry outside. It was a clear and chilly autumn night. Josh stepped out onto the back verandah and looked up at the stars. If his dad were here he would point out his favourite football constellations. 'There are the goalposts,' he would say, 'and there's the ref's whistle.' Finally, he would smile and whisper, 'Look, Josh, there's you scoring a try for Australia.'

Fat chance of that, thought Josh. *I can't even score a try for the Ravens.*

A moment later Harry returned from the darkness, holding a tennis ball in his mouth.

What's the point? thought Josh. 'Sorry, boy, not tonight.' Josh went inside and closed the door. Perhaps playing footy wasn't going to be as easy as he had first thought.

6
THE SURPRISE GUEST

'Okay, lads, gather round,' called Coach Steve.

It was training day for the West Hill Ravens and the team had just finished their warm-up laps around the field. The boys came and sat around Coach behind the goal-posts. Josh sat off to the side. No one had mentioned the dropped pass, but he still felt guilty. He was sure no one had forgotten the reason behind the team's opening-game loss.

'All right, who remembers what I said at training last week?' asked Coach Steve.

'You said Blake was a goose,' said Ravi.

'Yes, I did say that and for good reason,' replied Coach. 'You should never run around with your trackpants on your head. It's dangerous. But that's not what I'm talking about.'

'Oh, I remember. You said you would buy us pizza if we made the finals,' said Tai.

'Yay! Pizza!' cried the team.

'Ah, no, I didn't say that. I think I would remember,' Coach Steve said sternly.

Tai shrugged. 'That's what I heard.'

'Well, you heard wrong. If you lot can't remember, I guess I'll have to remind you. Last week I promised you a surprise guest at training today.'

'Oh yeah, now I remember,' said Blake.

Coach smiled broadly. 'Maybe you remember me telling you that when I lived up north as a boy I played footy for –'

'Australia!' cried Tai.

Coach shook his head. 'Stop interrupting, or you'll be running another lap around the oval. Now, as I was saying, as a kid I played footy for –'

'Hey, look – a taxi!' Blake pointed over to the car park. Within seconds the boys were all on their feet, trying to get a look.

'He's here,' said Coach Steve.

'Who's here?' asked Tai and Blake and Azza and Ravi.

But Josh didn't need to ask. He recognised his hero straight away. 'It's –'

'Billy Slater,' finished Coach Steve. 'We used to play footy together, and I knew he was in town for a game, so I asked him to give the team a special training session.'

'OMG! Billy Slater's gonna train *us*?' asked Azza.

'Yep!' Coach Steve waved for Billy to join them. The whole team swarmed around Billy and began asking a thousand questions all at once.

'What's it like to win a grand final?' asked Tai.

'What's it like to play for Australia?' asked Azza.

'How many tries have you scored?' asked Liam.

'And how many tries have you saved?' asked Blake.

'How much money do you get paid?' asked Corey.

'Corey, that's a bit personal,' warned Coach Steve.

'But that's what I was gonna ask, too,' said Cameron. 'Is it a million dollars?'

'Cameron!' yelled Coach Steve.

Billy chuckled. 'How about you guys ask one question at a time and I'll try to answer them all.'

Josh was the only one who wasn't asking questions. He was still in shock. His all-time footy hero was standing right there in front of him.

Coach Steve walked up beside Josh. 'I thought you'd be a bit more excited. Aren't you a fan of Billy's?'

Josh nodded. He did want to ask Billy a question, or at least tell him he was a big fan. Instead, his mouth just hung open like one of those laughing clowns you throw ping-pong balls at in carnivals.

Coach Steve whistled to get their attention. 'How about we show Billy what we can do?'

The boys all cheered and ran towards the field.

Suddenly, the elephant-sized butterflies were back. As Josh stood in line, waiting to run up to take a pass from his hero, all he could see was the ball crashing to the ground. To make matters worse, he had Corey breathing down his neck.

'Don't drop it this time, butter-fingers,' Corey hissed in his ear.

Josh ran towards Billy. *Don't drop it. Don't drop it. Please don't drop it!*

When Billy slipped him a simple pass, Josh reached out his hands to catch the ball and . . . it slipped right through them.

'Never mind, you'll get the next one,' Billy said with a smile.

Josh turned and slinked away. *Could it get any worse?*

'I knew you'd drop it,' said Corey. 'Why do you even bother?'

Tears sprang to Josh's eyes. Not wanting anyone to see him upset, he turned around and ran.

7
BACKYARD HERO

'Things look pretty desperate for the Ravens here, down by two with less than a minute on the clock.'

'It's their last-chance miracle play, all right, Roy. But will their prayers be answered?'

'We're about to find out as McGill takes the tap. He gets the ball out to the five-eighth, who dummies and gets a great ball away to the fullback. Cotter streaks away. He's just got the cover defence to beat.

They're closing in on him. He needs some support. There's no one there. Looks like the Ravens will come away empty-handed . . .

'Hang on. Here comes the new kid, Josh Brown, from out of nowhere. Cotter tosses it over the heads of the defence and . . . What a magnificent take from Brown! He's into the gap. Shut up shop, they won't get him now. It's try time!'

'That was all class from the winger. What a bright future this lad has, Roy.'

'That's putting it lightly, Mike!'

Josh climbed out of the back garden. He dusted off the leaves he'd collected from diving to score a try right behind his mum's favourite azaleas.

Harry was running in circles and barking excitedly. He loved to be involved in Josh's backyard games of footy, even if he rarely made a convincing tackle.

There's nothing like commentating a bit of fantasy footy to make you feel better, thought Josh. And he really needed it after the way training had finished. He'd spent the rest of the afternoon hiding in the change sheds.

When Coach Steve had asked if he was okay at the end of training, Josh told him that he wasn't feeling well, which wasn't that far from the truth.

The only good thing to come from it was the news that Billy Slater was going to be the Ravens Under 11s mentor for the year. Coach explained that a mentor was someone who gave extra advice and tips, and that Billy would be helping out when he wasn't busy with his playing commitments.

'Hmmm, looks like someone fancies their form,' came a croaky voice from behind.

Josh turned around, his cheeks flushing a bright pink. 'Oh, hi Grandad. I didn't realise you were there.'

'You need to be careful you don't ruin those flowers, or your mum will have your head.' Grandad's eyes twinkled. 'Why don't we head over to the park? I can show you a few things from my day, when people *really* knew how to play footy.'

Josh thought back to when he had 'practised' with his grandad once or twice before, and how it had ended badly both times. The old man had a bit of a quick temper. 'Um, I'm a bit tired. Maybe some other time.'

'Oh.'

Josh could see the disappointment in his grandad's face. Suddenly, he felt guilty.

'Well, let me know if you ever want some tips. I used to be pretty good back in the day.'

'Okay,' Josh said quickly.

Grandad opened his mouth as if to say something else but stopped himself. Then he just nodded and headed back to his flat, a little converted garage that sat alongside the main house.

He had lived with them since Josh's grandmother had passed away four years ago. Josh used to love going over there when he was younger. He'd sit on his grandad's couch and watch *ABC4Kids* for hours. But he didn't go there much anymore. His grandad was always complaining, usually about the government or teenagers. It could get a bit depressing listening to all that yelling at the radio or the TV.

Josh watched his grandad through the window of his flat. He was standing beside his kitchen sink, staring at the kettle.

Maybe I should have gone to the park, thought Josh, heading back to the house. *It's not like I can get much worse.*

8
GRUMPY OLD MAN

Saturday came and the Ravens were set to play against their local rivals, the Craxton Comets.

Josh and Grandad headed off to the game. This time, Mum had to stay home because Chloe had an ear infection. Josh felt like *he* was coming down with an ear infection after listening to his sister cry non-stop for hours the night before. He was so tired from being up all night that he had completely forgotten to be nervous about the game.

That all changed about ten minutes before kick-off, when he was taping up his boots. The elephant-sized butterflies were back, and this time it felt like they were playing Twister in his large intestine.

Despite his tummy troubles, Josh started the first half reasonably well. When the Comets' lightning-fast centre came galloping down the sideline towards him, Josh stood his ground. As the centre tried to sidestep him, Josh threw himself at the centre's leg. Josh held on, refusing to let go even as he slid down and caught a boot square in the face.

The centre fell to the ground before getting the pass away. Josh managed to pull himself up and quickly get into position as

marker. He could already feel the side of his face swelling up.

Azza, the Ravens hooker, jogged over as cover defence. 'Good tackle, Josh.'

Josh grinned, chuffed at the compliment from the best defensive player on his team.

'That's it, Joshie! Great work, son! They can't run without their legs,' Grandad called from the sideline.

What is he talking about? Of course they can't run without their legs. Who can? Josh wondered. Sometimes his grandad said the strangest things.

But the tackle wasn't the only good thing Josh did in the first half. He made two decent runs from dummy half and even got a good pass away to Poppa, who made a powering bust up the middle. This gave the Ravens the field position to grab their first try two tackles later.

All was going well – until the fight. Josh heard it before he saw it.

'Come on, Ravens, make 'em eat dirt!'

Grandad had called cheerily from the sideline.

A burly Comets supporter with a ginger beard responded, 'Get it out wide, Comets! The winger's got nothin'!'

'Nothing? That's my grandson you're talking about, mate,' Josh's grandad shot back.

What is he doing? thought Josh. *Can't he see that guy is at least six foot two and has biceps as big as basketballs?!*

'I'm not your mate, *mate*,' snorted Gingerbeard.

Josh watched in horror as his grandfather turned to face Gingerbeard. 'Is that right?'

This was terrible. The Comets were only a few metres away from the tryline, but Josh couldn't take his eyes off the trouble happening off field.

His grandad looked about half the size of Gingerbeard and was probably twice his age. Yet there he was, facing off with the Comets supporter.

'That's right. And your grandson *sucks*. Didn't you ever teach him how to play footy?' jeered Gingerbeard.

'No, I leave that to his coach. But I'm sure I could teach *you* a lesson or two,' said Grandad.

The rest of the team returned to the tryline. 'Josh, get back in line!' yelled Liam. But Josh wasn't listening. His eyes were glued to Gingerbeard.

Moments later, a Comets player slipped through the yawning gap in the Ravens' defence, where Josh should have been standing, and scored a try in the corner. Josh barely noticed. His eyes were wide with terror as he watched Grandad and Gingerbeard go head-to-head.

'Can you two zip it? I'm trying to watch my kid play,' said a lady nearby. She was holding a cup of coffee in one hand and a chihuahua in the other.

'Mind your own business,' said Gingerbeard, dismissing her with a wave.

This wasn't appreciated by the lady's chihuahua. It growled, arched its back into attack mode and then leapt at Gingerbeard's head.

The lady's coffee went flying. 'No, Fifi!' she yelled. 'Get down! Naughty dog!'

Gingerbeard went sprawling towards Grandad, who nimbly stepped out of the way. This set off a chain reaction, the likes of which had never been seen at an Under 11s rugby league match. Especially not during the second game of the season.

Gingerbeard quickly recovered and lunged at Fifi, but ended up colliding with another Comets fan. The unsuspecting man let out a high-pitched squeal and stumbled over his own esky. Josh watched in horror as the man fell back, landing on a table where two big-haired ladies in Comets tracksuits were sitting. Raffle tickets, notes and coins sprayed into the air.

People rushed from everywhere to help the ladies. Their immaculate hair and make-up was now besmirched with stray raffle tickets and clumps of grass. The poor Comets supporter who had been caught in the tussle was rubbing his backside and yelling at Gingerbeard. Meanwhile, Grandad stood there scowling his grumpy-old-man scowl and accepting absolutely no responsibility for the mayhem.

The game was temporarily halted while

Gingerbeard, Fifi and Fifi's owner were escorted from the grounds. A stern-looking club official advised Josh's grandad that it may be best if he removed himself from the supporters' area for 'unruly conduct'.

After an initial protest, which included Grandad claiming discrimination against the elderly, he finally agreed to leave. 'When you're finished, Josh, I'll be waiting in the car. God forbid I should watch my own grandson play a game of football and show a little support from the sideline.'

Josh closed his eyes and pretended he was invisible.

It didn't stop him from hearing his grandad's final rant to no one in particular as he made his way to the car park. 'You know you're ruining it for the kids! The greatest game in the world and you're ruining it. No wonder they all want to play soccer!'

Josh wanted to shrivel up and disappear into the ground.

Unfortunately, he didn't.

9
BENCHED

'Well, that was an *interesting* first half,' said Coach Steve.

Josh buried his head in his hands. The first half hadn't improved after his grandad was asked to leave. Naturally, he'd found it a little hard to focus. In all, Josh put down three perfectly good passes. He didn't even get his hands on them – one hit him square in the face, leaving a bright red mark. It was probably a big reason why the Ravens were still behind on the scoreboard.

'But despite all the distractions,' continued Coach Steve, and Josh wondered if Coach was looking at him, 'we are only down by four. We can still win this. Sure the Comets have a few good players, but I think we can take 'em. Let's just play as a team and hang onto those passes out there. If we do that, maybe we can notch up our first win of the season.'

Coach nodded to the boys, and they all knew what was coming. 'Ravens . . .' Coach started flapping his arms wildly, and the whole team cracked up before joining in. 'Let's fly!' yelled Coach Steve, and all the boys cheered and whooped. They could always count on Coach to make himself look ridiculous for the good of the team.

Even Josh felt a little better, or he did until Coach called him over for 'a chat'. Josh didn't like the sound of that.

'Listen, mate,' began Coach, 'you had a good run out there but I might get you to sit out this half so I can give Ravi a go, okay?'

Ravi Rangarajan was the Ravens' only reserve. He was a big football fan but had never played the sport before, and he was terrible at it. Ravi was the only player on the team who dropped the ball more than Josh.

'You're benching me?' Josh asked glumly.

'This is just a rest, mate. You did take a ball pretty hard to the head. Don't worry, you'll be back out there next week,' said Coach Steve, ruffling Josh's hair.

But as Josh watched the second half from his spot on the wooden bench, he started to wonder if maybe this was his new position in the team – especially when Ravi managed to catch a pass. He did run in the wrong direction, of course. But after being shouted at by his teammates, Ravi eventually turned around and ran the right way.

The Ravens gained the upper hand in the second half, scoring three tries to one by the time the final whistle blew. Coach Steve's talk had done the job, and the Ravens won their first game of the season, no thanks to Josh.

When Josh climbed into the car, he was beginning to think his footy-playing days were numbered.

'So you had a win, hey?' Grandad put aside his paper and turned on the ignition.

'Yep, 16–10,' mumbled Josh.

'Good for you.'

'Thanks.'

'Can you believe that club, kicking me out of the spectators' area? It's not like I threw any punches.'

'Yep.' Josh's mind was no longer on his grandad's sideline antics. He was too busy thinking about his own performance. His cheek still stung from where the football had smacked him in the face, and his lip was swollen from the boot he'd copped in the tackle.

Maybe I'm just not cut out to be a footballer, thought Josh. As if to confirm this, the car hit a bump and Josh's face vibrated with pain.

'Blasted potholes!' grumbled Grandad.

Josh stared at the grey road ahead. All the way home he wondered one thing: *What's wrong with me?*

10
THE YIPS

'I think it might be a case of the yips,' concluded Billy.

'The what?' asked Josh, still a little dumbstruck that Billy Slater was giving him advice about football. This might just be the greatest day of his life, but it certainly hadn't started that way.

When Josh had seen that Billy Slater was there to train the team, he'd been both excited and completely terrified. Those dreaded elephant butterflies rose from the dead. But this time they were zombie-elephant butterflies.

And that's how Josh ended up spending the first half of training in the change sheds.

'Um, Josh? Are you in here, mate?'

Josh gulped. 'Just a second . . .' he called back, and quickly flushed the toilet. The truth was that his stomach had been fine for twenty minutes. He had been sitting in the cubicle for all that time wondering if he should go outside and face the barrage of Corey's put-downs about stuffing up an easy pass.

Josh sheepishly emerged, trying to think of an excuse for missing the first half of training.

'How are you doing?' asked Billy.

Josh looked at the ground and gave a tiny shrug.

'That good, huh?'

Josh shrugged again.

'Steve said you had a tough game on the weekend,' Billy said with a concerned smile.

'I guess.'

'Feel like talking about it?' asked Billy. He pointed to the narrow wooden bench on the sidelines.

Josh nodded and sat down on the bench. Taking a deep breath, he explained everything that had happened in the game against the Comets. And after that, he explained what had happened at training the week before and when he had blown a certain try in the first game of the season.

'Not much fun to stuff up when everyone's watching, is it?' asked Billy.

'Not so much.'

Billy nodded. 'Yep, I know that feeling.'

'But . . .'

'But what? You don't think professional footy players get embarrassed when they make a mistake in front of thousands of fans?' asked Billy.

'But you *never* make a mistake. You're Billy Slater.'

'Of course I do. Everyone has their bad days. Believe me, I've had some shockers,' said Billy.

'Not like me. I can't even catch the ball anymore. Whenever I have to catch a pass I get nervous and my hands don't work,' said Josh, clenching his hands into fists.

And that's when Billy suggested that Josh was suffering from the yips. But Josh had no idea what Billy was talking about.

'The yips are when you worry so much about not being able to do something that your body forgets how to do it,' explained Billy. 'It happened to me one season when I dropped a bomb in the very first game. Every time after that, when a bomb went up, I'd think about dropping it. And then I would drop it.'

'So, how'd you fix it?' asked Josh.

'That's the tricky bit. The key is to relax, keep a clear mind and eventually it just goes away.'

'Just goes away? But how?' asked Josh. The yips sounded like a terrible disease, and he had been hoping Billy would be able to give him an instant cure. This was like being told by the doctor to drink plenty of fluids and get some rest.

'It just does. You just need one or two good passes to get your confidence back,' said Billy. 'Why don't we chuck around the footy and see if some of the passes stick? It beats hanging out in the change sheds, right?' Billy said with a grin.

'Okay.'

Josh and Billy headed over to the corner of the field while Coach Steve ran tackling drills with the rest of the team.

'So, the trick is to never, ever, ever take your eyes off the ball,' instructed Billy.

He threw Josh pass after pass. Easy ones

at first, then difficult ones – at Josh's hands, legs and over his head. Hard ones, fast ones, floating, spiralling passes and even flick passes. Josh didn't catch them all, but he caught most of them.

As the sun disappeared behind the hills and the sky turned pink, Josh began to feel better. He was having fun, and he knew that he could catch a pass. He could catch a lot of passes, in fact. He just had to remember this during the next game.

That was going to be the tricky bit.

11
THE EMPTY CHAIR

'Wow, a one-on-one passing session with Billy Slater. Lucky you! If I didn't hate his team so much, I'd be impressed.'

Josh squinted at the blurry image on his mum's laptop. 'Dad, how can you hate the most awesome team ever? They've won *nine* of their last ten games!'

'Well, son, it's just like me and Grandad – he's a dyed-in-the-wool footy fan and he's never had much time for my team, either. I guess the three of us will never see eye to eye on footy, which is probably not a bad thing. It makes footy season far more interesting, if you ask me.'

'Died in the woods? What does that mean?'

'Not died in the woods. D-Y-E-D – dyed in the wool, as in the dye used to colour wool, which you can never get out. Once you choose a footy team, it's for life. Mine might not be going too well at the moment, but I'm not about to switch to a different team just because they win a premiership. I'd rather die in the woods!'

Josh groaned. 'Dad, your jokes are terrible.'

'All dad jokes are terrible. Speaking of which, how is your grandad? Mum said there was some kind of problem at the game last weekend.'

'He's okay, I guess. He's just always yelling stuff from the sideline. Dad, it's embarrassing.'

'That's your grandad for you. My ears are still ringing from the last game we went to. But no one knows more about footy than your grandad. You should spend some one-on-one training time with him.'

Josh wasn't really keen to spend more time with his grandad than he had to. He was just too grumpy.

'I'd better go now, Josh. Look after your mum and Chloe for me, okay?'

'Okay.' Josh paused, not wanting to

sound too much like a little kid. 'Dad . . . when are you coming home?'

His dad frowned and cleared his throat. 'Soon, I hope. Good luck with the game on Saturday. Score a try for me.'

'I'll try,' said Josh, but he wasn't feeling very confident.

Then the laptop screen went black and his dad was gone again.

Josh, his mum and Grandad sat at the table and ate in silence. His mum seemed angry. Josh wondered if it was because his dad couldn't say when he was coming home.

The only one doing any talking was Chloe. But since Josh didn't speak 'baby', he had no idea what Chloe's various aahs, goos and gurgles meant. Maybe she had some good advice about beating the yips. She certainly looked relaxed, sitting in her highchair with a river of drool flowing freely from her bottom lip.

As Josh sat there watching his baby sister drool and his grandad gnaw enthusiastically on a lamb cutlet, he couldn't help but notice his dad's empty chair. Josh wondered if he would still have the yips if his dad was around to take him to footy. *He* wouldn't shout out embarrassing things from the sideline and be asked to leave the ground.

Maybe it's just as well that Dad's away, thought Josh. *At least he doesn't have to see me fumble a try.*

'Lovely lamb cutlets, Annie,' Grandad said, breaking the long silence.

Josh's mum smiled, but the smile disappeared when she glanced at Josh's plate. He had barely touched his dinner. For some reason he didn't feel very hungry.

12
WAR OF THE WORDS

Josh woke that Saturday to the sound of rain. *Great, that's all I need – a wet, slippery football! This is not going to be fun.*

It was still pouring when Josh and his grandad pulled into the Ravens home ground for Round 3 against the reigning premiers, the Kingsville Destroyers.

'Nice weather . . . for ducks,' Grandad said with a chuckle.

Josh winced. His dad was right – all dad

jokes are bad, but grandad jokes are the worst.

'Remember, Josh, wet weather means tough football.' Grandad slid one arm and then the other into a weathered yellow raincoat. 'You just have to guts it out and tackle, tackle, tackle. There won't be many tries today, so whoever gets over the line will probably win. Good luck out there, I'll be cheering for ya.'

That was the one thing Josh was worried about. Well, that and dropping the ball.

The mini-league games had been cancelled but all other age groups were to go ahead as scheduled. When the Ravens Under 11s ran onto the field, the rain was still beating down. If anything, it was coming down harder than ever.

Despite his fears of being benched again, Josh was in the starting line-up. That could have been due to the fact that Ravi hadn't even shown up. His parents had probably assumed the game would be called off. But this was rugby league. If the council didn't close the ground, it was game on.

In the team line-up before the game, Josh could barely see two feet in front of him. But one thing he did notice was the size of the Destroyers players. Some of them were *enormous*. They looked like they were in Year 9, not Year 5.

Josh couldn't tell if it was just the rain, black clouds and bad light, but he could have sworn that some of the players had stubble on their chins.

Once the game was underway, Josh realised that his grandad was right. It *was* nice weather for ducks. There was a family of them swimming around in the lake that was forming behind the in-goal area.

And there wasn't much chance of catching the ball in the blinding rain, let alone scoring. Not to mention the mind-numbing cold. Josh felt like his face was being stabbed by a thousand tiny needles and he could barely feel his feet in his waterlogged boots.

Guts it out, Josh, he could hear Grandad's voice in his head. *Easy for him to say*, thought Josh. *He's standing on the sideline in a raincoat.*

Of course, Josh's grandad was the only supporter dedicated enough to brave the rain. Every other spectator or official was standing under the eaves of the tuckshop and change sheds, or waiting in their car. His grandad was out there all alone, yelling words of encouragement to get Josh through the toughest playing conditions of his very short footballing career. Things like:

'Careful – don't drop it!'

'Courage, lad, it's only mud!'

'It's not a tackle if it doesn't hurt!'

It wasn't particularly helpful advice, so Josh thought about what Billy had told him. *Relax. Keep a clear mind.*

But Grandad's voice fought back. *Guts it out. Tackle. Tackle. Tackle.*

Soon there was a war of words inside Josh's head that was almost as loud as the rain smashing down on him.

GUTS IT OUT.

RELAX.

TACKLE. TACKLE. TACKLE.

KEEP A CLEAR MIND.

TACKLE. TACKLE. TACKLE.

EVENTUALLY, IT JUST GOES AWAY.

But how?

COURAGE, LAD. IT'S ONLY MUD.

But . . .

RELAX.

But . . .

TACKLE. TACKLE. TACKLE.

I can't.

CLEAR YOUR MIND.

Josh could see the giant Destroyers winger powering towards him. He had

never seen a bigger player, and this wasn't a forward, either. It was his opposite number.

With only a split second to react, Josh decided the best thing to do was to listen to both voices in his head. He relaxed, braced himself for impact, cleared his mind and then launched himself like a human missile at the colossus running at full steam towards him.

The last thing he saw was a very large set of kneecaps. Then everything went black.

13
DOWN THE DRAIN

'Josh? Honey, are you going to be much longer? Lunch is almost ready.'

Josh didn't have the energy to answer his mother. He sat in the bathtub, looking down at his battered body and the mud mingling with the water. It had been a tough game, all right. He'd recovered from the tackle by the giant Destroyers winger, although he had been left with a large black bruise from colliding with a leg that had felt as hard as concrete. But the game hadn't got any easier.

His grandad was right about another thing. It wasn't a high-scoring game. In the end the Destroyers won the day 8–0.

Even though Coach Steve had told the boys how proud he was of them all for playing so well in such terrible conditions, Josh didn't feel much pride. He'd hardly touched the ball, and when he had, it had slipped right out of his hands like soap. Maybe it was the rain or maybe it was the yips, but his ball-handling skills were still disastrous.

His body was aching, his head was throbbing and he felt very, very tired. Was this what playing rugby league was really like? *Maybe I'm not meant to play footy, after all*, thought Josh.

'Josh, did you hear what I said? Lunch is ready.'

'I'm coming!' Josh shouted back.

'All right, no need to get snippy,' his mum replied.

Josh felt bad. His mum didn't deserve to be yelled at. It wasn't her fault he wasn't good at football. She hadn't wanted him to play in the first place.

As he climbed out of the blackened bath-water, Josh realised what he had to do. He removed the plug and watched the water and sludge whirl down the plughole with a high-pitched groan.

At training on Tuesday he would tell Coach that he was quitting the team.

14
BILLY'S ADVICE

When Josh arrived at training, the sky was a bright, blazing blue and the only signs of the weekend rain were a few shallow puddles on the soft, squishy ground. The rest of the team was already out in the middle of the field playing a pre-training game of footy. They were running and yelling and calling to each other to pass it and kick it without a care in the world.

How do they do it? Josh wondered. They didn't look like they had any zombie-elephant-butterfly issues. They all just looked like they were having fun.

When he got out to the middle of the field, a few of the boys greeted him with a friendly nod.

'Wanna play, Josh?' asked Liam. 'We need one more on our team.'

'You guys can have him. He's hopeless!' said Corey.

'Corey, don't be slack!' Liam turned to Josh. 'Just ignore him.'

'What? I'm just being honest,' Corey shot back.

Josh could feel his cheeks turning beetroot-red. 'It's okay. I probably won't be staying long. I'm just looking for Coach,' he said quickly.

'He's not here yet,' said Liam. 'Why can't you stay for training, anyway?'

'Um, I'm probably going to have to quit the team,' announced Josh.

'Typical!' said Corey.

'Quit the team? Why?' asked Liam.

Josh had to think for a minute. Why was he quitting? 'Just a bit too busy. I've got a lot of stuff going on.'

'What kinda stuff?' asked Corey.

Josh gazed intently at a tuft of grass in front of him. 'Nothing interesting. Just a lot of stuff to do. So . . .'

'But we need you,' said Liam. 'We only have Ravi as reserve and . . .' Liam looked over at Ravi, who was carefully lining up to kick a football. He managed to miss the ball and fall over at the same time. 'He's just not that good.'

Corey gave a snort. 'He's terrible!'

'But you just said *I* was hopeless,' said Josh.

'You are!' said Corey. 'No offence.

But maybe if you actually stuck around at training, instead of disappearing all the time, you might get better.'

'Corey has a point – you have missed a bit of training,' said Liam. 'Do you really want to quit?'

'Who's quitting?' asked a voice behind them.

The boys turned around to find Billy Slater standing there.

'Hi Billy, where's Coach?' asked Corey.

'Steve couldn't make it today, he's having car trouble. He asked me to fill in for him,' said Billy. 'So, what's this about someone quitting?' he asked, looking at Josh.

'Well, it's just . . . I'm really . . .' Josh began awkwardly.

'He's too busy, he's got *stuff* to do,' said Corey.

'Corey, Liam, why don't you two grab the training kit and set up some markers so we can run drills?' said Billy. 'I'd like to talk to Josh for a sec.'

'Okay,' said Liam.

Billy waited until the rest of the team was out of earshot. 'All right, so what's all this rubbish about quitting? Has this got anything to do with what we talked about the other day?'

'Sort of,' said Josh. He turned to Billy, his eyes bright with unwelcome tears. 'I'm just not cut out for footy. At the rate I'm going, I'll never score a try.'

Billy raised an eyebrow. 'Score a try?

Is that the only reason you're playing? You know some players go their whole careers and never score a try.'

'Yeah, forwards. But wingers are supposed to score tries, aren't they?'

'Josh, you don't have to score a try. You just have to . . . *try*. Have a go, you know? It's no wonder you keep dropping the ball when you're worried about whether you're going to score or not. Don't over-think it.'

'But *how* do I do that?' asked Josh.

Billy thought for a moment. 'Maybe you could try a tip my mum gave me.'

Josh looked up in surprise. 'Your mum?'

'Yes, my mum. When I was having a problem with catching bombs it was my mum who fixed it. She told me to imagine catching something I would never drop,' said Billy.

'So, what did you imagine?' asked Josh, intrigued.

Billy grinned. 'Mum's lamb roast. There's no way I'd drop that!'

'And it worked? Catching a lamb roast?'

'Every time,' said Billy. 'Look, Josh, I'm not saying that you shouldn't quit. But quit because you don't want to play anymore. Don't quit because you're scared you're going to drop the ball or not score. Okay?'

Josh thought about it for a long moment. Was he just scared of failing? Did he still want to play footy? 'Okay,' he said finally.

'Good. Now, let's do some drills,' Billy said with a laugh.

And Josh did. And he had fun. And he didn't drop the ball, not once.

15
REALITY CHECK

When Josh arrived home after training, his head was buzzing. For the first time in weeks, he remembered why he'd wanted to play football. He LOVED it. He loved watching footy and he loved playing footy. It was like someone had switched on a light in his brain. He didn't have to score. He didn't even have to catch the ball. He just had to try.

Josh rushed into the kitchen.

'Waaaaaaaaahhhhhh!'

A familiar sound filled his ears. Chloe was screaming in her highchair, but Josh didn't let that dampen his enthusiasm. 'Mum, are you going to watch me play on Saturday? 'Cause I think it would be really good if you came,' he blurted out excitedly.

Mum looked up, surprised. 'I thought you were quitting the team?' She stirred Chloe's stinky baby food and then tasted some to check the temperature.

'Quitting the team?' echoed Grandad, lowering his newspaper. 'Why are you quitting the team?'

'I'm not quitting,' Josh quickly replied.

'You told me you were,' said Mum.

'Nope, no one's quitting,' repeated Josh.

'You'd better not be quitting after I bought you those shoulder pads. They weren't cheap, you know,' declared Grandad. 'Anyway, no grandson of mine is a quitter!'

'I'm *not* quitting!' shouted Josh. He turned to his mum. 'That's why I want to know if you can come on Saturday.'

'Josh, there's no need to shout, you'll upset your sister,' Mum said, raising her voice.

'But she's already screaming. And you're shouting, too!'

'Don't be cheeky to your mother, Josh,' said Grandad. 'Mind your manners.'

Josh let out a loud sigh. 'I just want to know if Mum's coming to the game! Is that too much to ask?'

'Well, Josh, it's very hard to get to the games when your father's away and I've got Chloe. It's hard to get anything done. You're just lucky that your grandfather is here to take you, or you wouldn't be able to play football at all.'

'You'd probably like that, wouldn't you?' spat Josh with all the spite he could muster.

'Oh, stop being ridiculous,' said Mum. 'It's not the *Josh Brown Show*, you know. We're a family. Stop being selfish and make yourself useful by feeding the dog, or *no one* will be going to the game on Saturday.'

Josh didn't say another word. Instead, he stormed out of the kitchen to sulk on the back step, with Harry by his side. 'Come on, boy, I'll get you some dinner,' Josh said to a hungry-looking Harry. 'At least you listen to me.'

As he gave Harry a final scratch under his chin Josh glanced up at the stars in the sky, but there were none to be found.

16
ROUND FOUR

There was an uncomfortable silence as Josh and his grandad headed to the ground for Round 4, against the Willamurra Wolves. His grandad wasn't listening to the radio for once. There was just the rattle of the motor and the low whistling of the autumn wind outside.

Josh stared out at the bleak grey sky. It was a dull, dreary day. And it was just him and Grandad. His mum had been up all night with Chloe, and she had still been in bed when they had left the house.

'So . . .' his grandad said, finally breaking the silence, 'your dad said you're embarrassed by my barracking at the games.'

Oh, great work, Dad. Thanks a lot. 'You spoke to Dad?'

'Last night.'

Josh could tell that Grandad wasn't happy. But he didn't sound grumpy, either. There was something in his voice that Josh hadn't heard before. He sounded hurt. 'Sometimes it's a bit . . . distracting when you yell stuff,' said Josh, trying to think of a nice way of putting it.

'That's all right, Josh. I get it. You don't need some old fool yelling out rubbish from the sidelines in front of all your teammates. I just want you to know that I only do it so you know someone is on your side. I just want you to be the best you can be.'

Josh felt awful. His grandad's voice sounded raspy and soft as if he were about to cry, and it was all his fault. 'I really don't mind that much – yell whatever you want. I'll wear earplugs.'

Grandad laughed. 'No need for that. Anyway, you won't have to worry today, because I have a little errand to run.'

'You won't be watching me?' Josh was surprised to find himself feeling disappointed rather than relieved.

'You'll be right, lad. Just know that every time you run out onto that field I'm already proud of you,' said Grandad, giving Josh the tiniest of smiles.

They pulled into the Wolves' home ground and Josh slowly climbed out of the car. He looked back at his grandad.

'Go on then. Get going.' Grandad paused for a moment. 'And, Josh, remember – it's just a little game of footy.'

Josh nodded and watched as the battered old Land Cruiser pulled out of the car park.

I guess I'm on my own then, thought Josh. He swung his backpack onto his shoulder and walked off to find his team.

17
TRY TIME

The Ravens Under 11s sat in the visitor change sheds, listening to Coach Steve's final instructions.

Josh could feel those familiar butterflies fluttering inside him, but he was determined not to let them win today. He glanced around at his teammates. They looked focused, ready. Some were tapping their boots on the ground or shaking their knees. Tai was bouncing a football against the wall. Perhaps they were all a bit nervous, too.

Josh began shaking his knees. It seemed to help a little. Soon he was stomping his boots on the ground as well.

After a few stretches and a pass of the ball, Coach said it was time to take the field.

Josh took a deep breath. *Just a little game of footy.*

Liam led them onto the field, and the family and friends on the Ravens' side cheered.

No one's cheering for me, Josh thought glumly. Then, from the corner of his eye, Josh noticed a familiar face. He broke into a smile and waved.

Billy gave him a fist pump in return. 'Try,' he mouthed, and Josh nodded. He was determined to.

The whistle blew and the game began.

The first half was hard. Both teams defended well. Josh wasn't the best at tackling, but he remembered the tips that Billy had given him at training and managed to make three good tackles.

When the Ravens won a scrum in the opposition half, it was the real moment of truth. Jack Monroe, the Ravens' lock, made a great bustling run up the right-hand side.

'Jack!' Josh called, running beside him.

Hearing his name, the forward glanced over his shoulder and spotted Josh. He floated a pass to Josh, just as he was tackled by the opposition. The pass was a high one, and Josh reached up to take it. He tried to imagine it was something important, something that he wouldn't drop. Then he was hit by the fullback, and the ball went bouncing away over the sideline.

Josh crumpled onto the ground. He could hear Corey from somewhere behind him. 'Told you he was hopeless!'

He felt a hand on his jersey, pulling him to his feet. 'Good try, Josh,' panted Liam. 'Keep it up.'

Josh got to his feet and dusted himself down. 'Thanks, Liam,' he said with a grin. *Maybe this* is *fun,* he thought

At half-time, the score was locked at 0–0.

The boys sat eating their orange quarters

in their half of the field. Josh was breathing hard. He had run flat out for the first half, and it felt good. But he knew it wasn't quite enough. Somewhere in the second half there was a pass with his name on it, and this time he would have to be ready.

As Coach Steve started waggling his arms to make his trademark 'Ravens, fly!' rev-up, Josh noticed a ray of sunshine poking through the clouds. Maybe it was a sign.

THOOOWEEEEEP!

The ref's whistle blew to start the second half, and the Ravens didn't exactly get off to the best start. Matthew Miller, the Miller twin whom the whole team had nicknamed 'Michael' simply because his brother's name was Jackson, dropped the ball from the kick-off. They weren't a minute into the half and the Wolves already had a set of six deep in the Ravens' territory.

After three repeat sets, the Ravens could hold out the Wolves no longer. When the Ravens' other winger, Nick Raco, and their fullback, Cameron, collided with each other in an attempt to ground a grubber kick, the Wolves scored in the corner. Suddenly, it was 4–0.

The Wolves missed the conversion from out wide and the Ravens knew they were still in it. But as the game went on, it didn't look like they would ever get the chance to score. The Wolves' defence was just too strong. They got off their line quickly and pushed back the Ravens with two-man tackles. The Ravens were struggling to even make it out of their own half.

With ten minutes left, a tired Wolves forward failed to get back the five metres in time and was caught offside. The Ravens received a penalty. This was their chance.

'Let's go, boys!' called Coach Steve, clapping his hands.

The Ravens took the tap. *This is it*, thought Josh. *The ball is coming to me. Any second now.*

Azza passed to Tai, who dummied and spun and off-loaded to Liam.

Fifteen metres.

Liam zigzagged and got an off-load to Jackson.

Ten metres.

Jackson ran straight and hard, then passed it to Corey, who turned to find Josh running outside him. Josh could tell that Corey wasn't keen to pass it to him.

Here goes nothing, thought Josh.

Five metres.

'Corey, I'm open!' Josh yelled.

Corey hesitated for a moment. Then he finally passed the ball to Josh, just as a defender dived at his waist.

It was a terrible pass – wide and high. As Josh raised his hands to catch the ball, he heard a familiar sound from the crowd.

'Waaaaaahhhhh!'

Josh would recognise that cry anywhere. It was Chloe. Josh no longer saw the ball floating towards him. Instead, he saw his baby sister tumbling through the air.

Two metres.

He plucked Chloe from the air and looked down to see the football in his hands.

Hey, it worked! thought Josh, just as two Wolves defenders leapt at him. But Josh was too fast for them. He dived for the line, the ball in his outstretched hands, and landed with a thud on the turf.

The crowd gasped.

Josh looked up to see the ball in his hands and his hands on the white line.

He was over! He had scored a try.

18
THERE'S ALWAYS NEXT WEEK

Before Josh could make it to his feet, his teammates piled on top of him in a celebratory stacks-on. They pulled him up and began ruffling his hair and high-fiving him.

Even Corey congratulated him. 'Well done, Brown. You didn't drop it.'

'Um, thanks, Corey . . . I guess.' Josh turned to the crowd and, sure enough, there was his mother and Chloe. They had made it, after all. But it wasn't just them – his dad and grandad were standing there as well, waving and cheering. *So this was the errand Grandad had to run!*

'On ya, Joshie! I knew you could do it!' shouted Grandad, and this time Josh wasn't embarrassed at all.

Standing right beside his family were Coach Steve and Billy, both of them grinning from ear to ear. Billy gave Josh a big thumbs-up.

As it happened, the Ravens didn't convert the goal and neither team managed to post any more points. By the time the final whistle blew, the score was locked at 4–4. It was a draw.

The team was disappointed, but as Josh shook hands with the other players, he didn't feel that bad that they hadn't won. The

Wolves had played just as well as they had, and a draw seemed like the fairest result.

Josh ran straight to his dad and hugged him so hard he almost knocked him over. 'I can't believe you came!' shouted Josh.

'I couldn't miss your first try, could I?' said his dad.

'With speed like that, it will be the first of many,' Grandad said, with a wink at Josh.

Josh tickled his sister. 'I owe it all to Chloe – she was my inspiration.'

'Well, in that case, maybe you can change her for me,' said Mum. 'She's left a little inspiration in her nappy for you.'

'Eww! Mum, that is so gross.'

His mum laughed. 'I know. But I am very proud of you, Joshie.'

Before Josh could think any more about the contents of his sister's nappy, Billy was standing next to him. 'Hey, Josh, you never told me that your grandfather is Keith "Bumper" Brown. The man's a living legend!'

'What, you mean *Grandad*?' asked Josh.

'He only played in one of the greatest grand finals of all time! My dad's always going on about it,' said Billy.

'You didn't tell me you played first grade, Grandad!' cried Josh.

His grandfather grinned and held up his hands. 'You never asked me.'

'After your performance today, maybe you'll follow in his footsteps, hey?' said Billy.

Josh sighed. 'We still didn't win.'

‘Well,’ said Billy, scratching his chin, ‘the thing about footy is, there’s always next week.’

‘Unless you’re still thinking about quitting?’ said Coach Steve.

Josh gave a sheepish grin. ‘Um, I think I’ll stick it out. I’m starting to get the hang of it.’

‘That you are, my boy. That you are,’ said Grandad. ‘Now, who wants to buy me a sausage sandwich? I’m starving.’

As Josh stood there in the presence of not one but two football legends, having just scored his first try ever, he thought to himself, *When it comes to footy, it probably doesn't get much better than this*.

Until next week, at least.

1. Fullback: Cameron 'C.C.' Cotter
2. Winger: Nick Raco
3. Centre: Blake 'The Fake' Vargas
4. Centre: Corey Wilson
5. Winger: Josh Brown
6. Five-Eighth: Tai Nguyen
7. Halfback: Liam McGill
8. Prop Forward: Junior 'Cannonball' Taafuli
9. Hooker: Ahmed 'Azza' Azzi
10. Prop Forward: Lucas 'Poppa' Popovic
11. Second Row: Matthew 'Michael' Miller
12. Second Row: Jackson Miller
13. Lock Forward: Jack Monroe

Reserve: Ravi Rangarajan

Coach: Steve Smith

PLAYER PROFILES

AGE: 10 WEIGHT: 42 kg

HEIGHT: 145 cm POSITION: Winger

An inexperienced but speedy player, what Josh lacks in confidence and size, he makes up for in heart. Josh is a great support player and, given a chance, he will tear away down the sideline. Expect lots of points from this galloping winger before the season is over – once he gets his ball-handling under control.

Josh's interests include football and his fave food is a classic barbecued sausage sandwich – don't forget the tomato sauce.

AGE: 10

HEIGHT: 160 cm

WEIGHT: 59 kg

POSITION: Prop Forward

Junior is the youngest player on the team, and he is also the biggest. His tackle-busting line breaks have earned him the nickname Cannon-ball. But don't be fooled by his size. This forward has some pretty handy ball skills and a tricky little flick pass, too. Junior can win a game almost single-handedly, but prefers to throw the ball around with his teammates and rely on his skill, rather than his size. When he's not breaking tackles, this unlikely rapper is busting rhymes. Word!

AGE: 11

HEIGHT: 152 cm

WEIGHT: 45 kg

POSITION: Centre

Corey's motormouth may get him into a bit of trouble with his teammates, but this fiery centre is the team's speed demon. Corey is a deadset try machine with a killer sidestep, although he does have a tendency to go 'one out' a little too often.

Besides playing footy, Corey helps his mum make ends meet by delivering Crazee Bargains catalogues. He's pretty handy on a skateboard as well.

Ravi is super-smart and can rattle off any footy statistic or piece of trivia about the game you can throw at him. Just don't throw him the football – his skills are a little on the under-developed side. But with a little confidence and coaching, Ravi's natural intelligence and enthusiasm for footy may convert to points on the board before the season ends.

Ravi is a self-confessed maths geek and prides himself on knowing more footy facts than a TV commentary team.

AGE: 10

HEIGHT: 147 cm

WEIGHT: 41 kg

POSITION: Reserve

He might be the team's smallest player but this pocket rocket half is the Ravens' engine. Without Liam calling the plays and driving his teammates forward, the Ravens would get nowhere. His lightning reflexes and natural instinct for the game make Liam the Ravens' MVP – most valuable player.

Liam's interests include footy, footy and more footy.

AGE: 11

HEIGHT: 140 cm

WEIGHT: 38 kg

POSITION: Halfback and Team Captain

BILLY'S TIPS

Tackling

The key point to tackling is safety first. You never want to put your head, neck or back into a dangerous position.

Key points

- When tackling head on, move towards the ball runner quickly in an upright position in order to cut down the space and time they have to manoeuvre.

- Bend your knees and drop your shoulder into the tackle, keeping your head tight against the player's hip, your chin up and neck straight.
- Wrap your arms tight around the player and drive with your legs to force the player to the ground.
- To practise tackling, run through the tackle sequence above with a friend in slow motion without any force, ensuring your head and neck are safely placed, tight against the player's body.
- Then try running the sequence a little quicker until you feel confident with getting your body in the right position.

Running Pass

Passing on the go takes timing and precision. Practising your passing is essential to building your confidence and ball-handling skills.

Key points

- When passing on the move, run with the ball held in both hands.
- A good grip is important. Keep your fingers spread in the middle of the ball and your thumbs on top of the ball.
- Make sure you pass in a backward motion to keep the receiver on side.
- As the outside foot is about to land, prepare to pass.

- Pass off both legs, starting the ball on your outside hip. Keep your eyes on the player receiving the ball, aiming the pass at his hands and chest area.
- Extend arms in the pass and swing arms through as you pass the ball to the receiver.

Catching a Pass

Catching a pass on the go can be tricky, espccially if the pass isn't perfect or if there's pressure from defenders.

Key points

- When you're about to receive a pass, raise your hands early in preparation, to provide a target for the passer.

- Your hands should form a W.
- Keep your hands up at around armpit height and keep your eye on the ball.
- Reach out for the ball and catch away from your body before drawing it into your chest.
- Practise passing drills by running alongside a friend or teammate.
- You can practise alone by making a chalk mark at chest height on a brick wall and aiming your running passes at the mark. Catching the ball on the rebound can be a fun challenge, too!

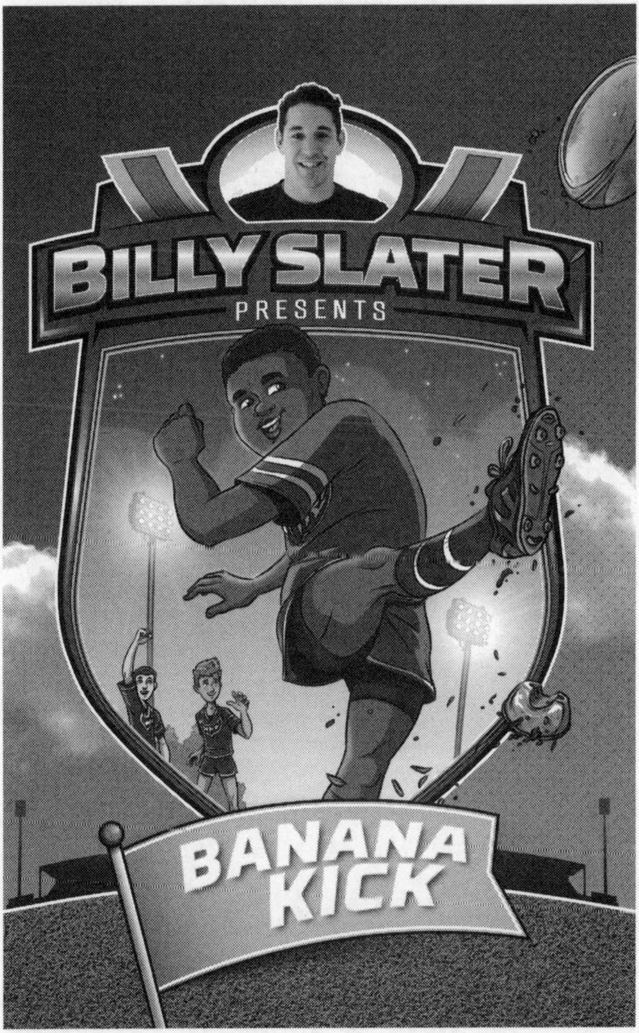

AVAILABLE NOW

LOOK OUT FOR THE NEXT BOOKS IN THE SERIES

SHOW AND GO

AND

CHIP AND CHASE

AVAILABLE AUGUST 2014